Catch That Cat Burglar!

"A couple of kittens from a brand-new litter disappeared yesterday from the River Heights Animal Shelter," Chief McGinnis said. "Know anything about it?"

"I didn't hear about any missing kittens," Pete told the officer. "I've got some new little ones myself, but I got them from a breeder named John Jones."

The police officer turned on his heel to leave the store. Nancy led her friends in a rush to catch up.

"Chief McGinnis," Nancy Drew called after him. "Can we help you find the missing kittens?"

The chief turned, grinning warmly. "You know, Nancy, I can always use help from you and your friends."

"Well then," George said happily, "let's get started."

NANCY DREW

#27 AND THE CLUE CREW®

Cat Burglar Caper

BY CAROLYN KEENE

ILLUSTRATED BY MACKY PAMINTUAN

SCHOLASTIC INC.
New York Toronto London Auckland
Sydney Mexico City New Delhi Hong Kong

ISBN 978-0-545-40563-8

Text copyright © 2010 by Simon & Schuster, Inc.
Illustrations copyright © 2010 by Macky Pamintuan.
All rights reserved. Published by Scholastic Inc., 557 Broadway, New York, NY 10012, by arrangement with Aladdin Paperbacks, an imprint of Simon & Schuster Children's Publishing Division. NANCY DREW and related logos are registered trademarks of Simon & Schuster, Inc. NANCY DREW AND THE CLUE CREW is a registered trademark of Simon & Schuster, Inc. SCHOLASTIC and associated logos are trademarks and/or registered trademarks of Scholastic Inc.

12 11 10 9 8 7 6 5 4 3 2   11 12 13 14 15 16/0

Printed in the U.S.A.   40

First Scholastic printing, September 2011

Designed by Lisa Vega
The text of this book was set in ITC Stone Informal.

CONTENTS

CHAPTER ONE: WHERE'S HANNAH? · · · · · · · · · 1

CHAPTER TWO: KITTEN-NAPPED! · · · · · · · · · · · 11

CHAPTER THREE: SUSPICIOUS SHELTER · · · · · · · · · 21

CHAPTER FOUR: QUICK QUESTIONS · · · · · · · · · · 33

CHAPTER FIVE: REAL RESEARCH · · · · · · · · · · · 41

CHAPTER SIX: THE PERFECT PLAN · · · · · · · · · 50

CHAPTER SEVEN: SEARCHING THE SUSPECTS · · · · · 57

CHAPTER EIGHT: KIND KITTENS · · · · · · · · · · · · 67

CHAPTER NINE: CAT CAPER CLOSED? · · · · · · · · 73

CHAPTER TEN: THE NOSE KNOWS · · · · · · · · · · 78

Cat Burglar Caper

ChaPTER ONE

Where's Hannah?

"I'm sooo bored . . . ," Bess complained as she flipped through the pages of an old magazine.

It was a beautiful day and eight-year-old best friends Nancy Drew, Bess Marvin, and George Fayne were hanging out in Nancy's bedroom with no real plans.

Nancy was splayed out on the floor, making a castle out of dominoes. "I'll do whatever you guys want to do," she said, momentarily distracted by a metal clanking sound coming through the open window. Blocking it out, Nancy continued building her guard tower.

"We need an adventure," George said, flopping

back over Nancy's bed so her short brown hair hung upside down.

Bess tossed the magazine aside. "I wish we had a mystery to solve. That would be exciting."

Even though Bess and George were cousins, they were very different from each other and hardly ever did the same thing. At that moment, however, the two girls both looked at their friend Nancy.

Nancy was a great detective. Bess and George often helped her solve mysteries. Together the three girls called themselves the Clue Crew and made their headquarters in Nancy's room.

"You never know when a mystery might happen," Nancy told them, carefully setting another domino on her stack.

Bess sighed. "Since we aren't investigating anything right now, we might as well go shopping."

George groaned. "Are you kidding?" She thought for a minute, then sat up and asked, "How about a movie instead?"

"Ugh, again?" Bess asked, standing up and tossing back her blond hair. She put her hands on her hips.

"How about this: We head downtown, see a movie, then go shopping afterward?" Nancy suggested, raising her head to look at her friends.

When neither of them responded, Nancy refocused on the dominoes, saying, "Or we could just stay here and do NOTHING all day."

At that, the girls both agreed to go to the movies and then shopping.

"Great!" Nancy popped up quickly, accidentally knocking into the tower she'd spent the past hour building. The girls watched as the dominoes fell in a wave. "Oh no," Nancy moaned, pressing her hands to her cheeks. Nancy was used to being a little clumsy, so it wasn't the first time she would have to start a project over. She immediately began thinking of ways to improve the castle. "I'll work on it again after we get back. Right now, we need a

ride downtown. Let's go find Hannah."

Hannah Gruen had been the Drew family housekeeper since Nancy was three years old. When Mr. Drew was at work, Hannah took care of Nancy and the household chores.

"Hannah!" Nancy called out as the girls entered the kitchen. It was the most logical place to find her because Hannah was an amazing cook.

"She's not here," Bess said, looking around. "I wonder where Hannah is."

The girls checked the living room, then Mr. Drew's study. No Hannah.

"Hmm." Nancy's detective skills were kicking in. "Let's see if she's in the garage." The girls walked outside through the open gate over to the garage. "That should have been closed," she muttered.

Hannah's car was parked in the garage, but still no Hannah.

"Where could she be?" Nancy wondered aloud.

"What's this?" George asked, scooping a white rag smeared with black grease off the driveway.

"Hmm," Nancy said, pushing a loose strand of reddish brown hair behind her ear. "Bess, your wish has come true. We've stumbled onto a mystery." Nancy thought about the square of cloth George discovered. "Hannah is always super neat and clean. She must have dropped this by accident. This rag is our first clue."

"Here's another clue!" Bess called from the garage. George and Nancy hurried over to where Bess stood by an open tool box. Bess knew a lot about tools and fixing things. "See?" Bess pointed at an empty space. "A lug wrench is missing."

"Huh?" George asked. "What's a lug wrench?"

"You use it for fixing tires," Bess answered.

Nancy fell quiet for a minute while her friends searched for more clues. Then she declared, "I know where Hannah is!"

George and Bess both looked at Nancy with a mixture of disbelief and awe, then followed as the detective led them back through the open gate. They crossed the front yard and walked over to Nancy's neighbor's house.

"Hey Mr. Seilsopour," Nancy greeted their new neighbor. Nancy didn't know him very well, but Hannah had told her that he was a mechanic and had come to River Heights to open his own car repair shop.

Hannah was very excited about Mr. Seilsopour's new shop. Not only was Hannah a great cook, a great nanny, and a great house-keeper, but she was also really good at repairing things.

Mr. Seilsopour peeked out at Nancy from under the hood of a very old, rusty pickup truck. He wiped his greasy hands on an oil-covered white rag, the exact same kind that George had found, and came over to meet Nancy's friends.

"Is Hannah here?" Nancy asked. Nancy had used her detective skills and put it all together: the open gate, the rag, and the missing wrench. She also remembered the clanging she'd heard as she lay on her bedroom floor earlier. Metal clanging, like someone working on a car . . . or a truck. When she put the clues together, Nancy was certain Hannah was nearby.

"Over here," a sweet voice greeted them from behind the truck. Nancy, Bess, and George went over and found Hannah working to put a brand-new front tire on the truck. "Hand me that lug nut, please," Hannah asked Nancy.

"Lug nut?" Nancy looked at George. George shrugged. Neither of them knew what Hannah was talking about.

Bess rolled her eyes and squeezed between her friends. She picked up the object Hannah wanted. "Here."

"Thanks, Bess," Hannah said.

"You sure seem to know a lot about tools," Mr. Seilsopour commented to Bess.

"Bess knows a lot about everything mechanical," George said proudly.

"Hannah came over to see this old truck I found at the junkyard," Mr. Seilsopour told the girls. "She kindly volunteered to help me fix it up."

"You're welcome to help us, if you want," Hannah extended an invitation to Bess.

Nancy thought that Bess's eyes were going to fall out of her head, she was so excited.

"Can I start now?" Bess asked, bouncing on her toes. "Right now?"

Mr. Seilsopour laughed. "That's exactly what Hannah asked!" At that, Hannah grinned.

"Hey wait, Bess, we're going to go downtown," George reminded her. She poked Bess in the side to bring her cousin back to planet Earth. "Movies. Shopping. Remember? We came over to ask Hannah for a ride."

Bess's face fell. She wanted to start on the truck immediately.

Hannah saw Bess's disappointed look. She wiped her hands and stood up. "This tire is done so I'm finished here for the day. I'll be happy to take you girls downtown."

"Bess," Mr. Seilsopour said, "Hannah's planning to come back over tomorrow. You can help us then, if you want."

"Yippee!" Bess said. "I can't wait."

"Well then," George said with a laugh, "the Mystery of Missing Hannah has been solved!"

"You never know when there might be another mystery," Nancy replied, tapping her pocket. "I'm bringing my detective's notebook along—just in case . . ."

Chapter Two

Kitten-Napped!

"That movie was awesome!" Bess exclaimed, tossing her popcorn container into a bin near the exit.

"At first I was so worried about the animals," George said with a shiver. "After the plane crash, the two dogs and cat went off by themselves, searching for help."

Nancy put an arm around George. "It all turned out well though," she said. "They crossed the mountain and found that woman who understood she needed to get rescue people to follow them back to the plane. It was so exciting."

"Yeah," George smiled thinking back over the

movie. "But I was on the edge of my seat when the beagle puppy fell into the river and the water was dragging her downstream." George clutched her heart dramatically and breathed a sigh of relief. "I'm glad that cat saved her. That was my favorite part."

"I loved that part too." Bess agreed. "That puppy was super cute with his big floppy ears and little wagging tail."

"Let's cross the street and look at the pets in Pete's Pets." Nancy suggested. "After that movie, I want to see some real cats and dogs."

Hannah walked the girls to the pet shop, then went next door to the hardware store to grab a few parts for Mr. Seilsopour's truck. "I'll meet you here in a half hour," she told the girls.

Pete was welcoming his customers at the door, showing off some puppies he was selling. "I knew families would want to adopt beagles after seeing that new movie," Pete told Nancy and the girls as they entered the shop.

"Cool," Bess said. She petted the puppy Pete

was holding on its fuzzy little head.

"There are more over there," Pete said, pointing toward the back of the store. "Plenty of puppies for everyone."

"Thanks, we'll take a look," Nancy said. Nancy already had a dog named Chocolate Chip, but she was happy to visit the shop's puppies.

"Look all you like," Pete said with a warm smile.

The girls headed to the back of the store, where the puppies were playing around in small pens. Two girls from school, Deirdre Shannon and Suzie Park, were already there, looking at the beagles.

"Hey, Nancy," Deirdre was holding one of the beagle pups in her arms. She showed it to Bess and George. "I'm going to ask my dad if we can adopt her," she said happily. "I'll call her Sunrise because she's got golden colored splotches. They remind me of clouds in the early morning sun."

"Cute name," Bess said. She knew that Deirdre didn't have any pets. "Do you think your dad'll let you have him?"

Deirdre was struggling to control the wiggly fellow, saying, "*Her.* And, I hope so."

Bess remarked, "Sunrise looks exactly like the puppy in the movie that we just saw."

"That's why I picked her. I saw the movie yesterday," Deirdre explained.

George agreed with Bess that Sunrise looked a lot like the movie dog, but Nancy thought that the famous dog had darker brown spots.

"What do *you* think, Suzie?" George asked.

Suzie tossed back her long, dark hair and shrugged. "I haven't seen the movie yet. I've been too busy." She pointed to the logo on the jacket she was wearing. The jacket was too big and very warm for such a nice day, but Suzie was obviously pleased to be wearing it. She stood up straight so Nancy could read the printing.

"River Heights Animal Shelter." Nancy noted that the words were right above a little picture of a dog and a cat, standing on their back legs, shaking paws.

"I've been volunteering at the shelter," Suzie said proudly. "I go there every day." Suzie then offered to show Deirdre a better way to hold the puppy. "I have a special technique," she claimed.

Deirdre tried to hand Suzie the squirmy little dog, but Suzie's slick jacket made holding the puppy difficult, so Suzie took off the coat and laid it on the floor.

Nancy, Bess, and George leaned in to see Suzie's holding technique. Suzie managed to settle the restless dog down, but when she handed the pup back to Deirdre, it got excited again and leaped out of Deirdre's arms, scampering across the store at full speed.

Bess and George rushed after the puppy. Nancy started to run too, but she slipped on Suzie's jacket and went sailing in a different direction, toward a sheet-covered cage tucked in a corner of the store.

"Aah!" Nancy exclaimed in surprise as she surfed across the slick floor. She grabbed at the cage intending to steady herself, but the sheet came off in her hands and Nancy crashed to the floor in a heap.

"Are you okay?" Suzie came hurrying over. She had the runaway puppy tucked under one arm. "I'm so sorry," she said, picking up the jacket with her free hand.

Nancy dusted herself off. "I'm fine," she said with a smile. "Your jacket is good for soft landings."

Suzie chuckled. "It's warm and cozy to *wear*, too." Suzie walked away, carrying the puppy back to Deirdre.

"Look!" Bess exclaimed, once she and George had caught up with Nancy. She was peering into the open-topped glass cage that Nancy had uncovered. Inside were two of the tiniest kittens that Nancy had ever seen. They looked like little, brown fuzz balls with wee, toothpick legs.

"I totally want a kitten!" Bess announced. "Aren't they adorable?" Nancy and George looked at Bess questioningly. She'd never even mentioned wanting a pet before.

Pete came over. "Those kittens aren't ready for adoption yet," he said, gathering up the sheet that had covered the cage. "They're too young."

"How old are they?" Nancy asked, looking into the cage, noticing that Pete had made them a nice bed out of old, torn blankets.

Pete explained. "They're only a few weeks old, so I'm still bottle-feeding them. Once they can feed themselves from a bowl, I'll put them up for adoption." He picked up one of the kitties. "It'll be a few more weeks." He held out the baby to show the girls. "I'm getting more from this

same litter. They'll be here in the next few days,
if you want to come in and see them, too."

"I really, really want a kitten," Bess said softly.
She looked up at Pete. "Can I hold one, please?"

Pete very tenderly moved the kitten from his
palm into Bess's. She smiled brightly as she ran
her thumb over the kitten's tiny back. But then—

"Achoo!" Bess sneezed. She pet the kitten once
more. "Achoo!" Bess sneezed
again. And again. And again.

Bess quickly handed the
kitten back to Pete. "I can't

believe it, but I think I might be allergic to cats!" Feeling sad, Bess stuck out her lower lip in a pout and said, "No fair. No kittens for me, I guess."

"Stick with dogs," Nancy told Bess as Pete put the kitten back in the cage with its sister and covered them up again with the sheet. "You can come play with Chocolate Chip any time." Bess smiled thankfully.

Just as the girls were getting ready to leave the shop, Chief McGinnis, head of River Height's police force, stopped by to talk to Pete.

"A couple of kittens from a brand-new litter disappeared yesterday from the River Heights Animal Shelter," Chief McGinnis said. "Know anything about it?"

"I didn't hear about any missing kittens," Pete told the officer. "I've got some new little ones myself, but I got them from a breeder named John Jones." The Chief nodded encouragingly so Pete continued. "His cat farm is called Kind Kittens. Mr. Jones owns some mother cats and brings me their babies to sell to nice families."

Pete walked to the front counter, reached beneath the register, and took out some official looking papers. He handed the documents to the officer.

Chief McGinnis glanced over Pete's papers before handing them back. "Okay," he said at last. "Let me know if you see or hear anything suspicious about kittens."

The police officer turned on his heel to leave the store. Nancy led her friends in a rush to catch up.

"Chief McGinnis," Nancy Drew called after him. "Can we help you find the missing kittens?"

The chief turned, grinning warmly. "You know, Nancy, I can always use help from you and your friends."

"Well then," George said happily, "let's get started."

"Finally! A real mystery to keep us busy," Bess said with a smile.

Nancy reached into her back pocket and pulled out her bright purple notepad and matching pen. "The Clue Crew is on the case!"

ChaPTER ThReE

Suspicious Shelter

The next morning Hannah drove Nancy, Bess, and George to the River Heights Animal Shelter, dropping them off in front. Nancy had scheduled a tour with Sandra Berman, the shelter director. Ms. Berman was a young woman with wild blond hair, pulled back into a ponytail.

"Good morning, ladies," Ms. Berman greeted them. Nancy noticed that there were black circles under Ms. Berman's eyes, like she hadn't had enough sleep. She was also carrying a cup of coffee bigger than any cup Nancy had ever seen.

"When Nancy arranged for the tour, she told me that you'd like to see the kittens first,"

Ms. Berman confirmed with the girls. She then mentioned how sad she was that two kittens were missing. "Baby kittens need a great deal of attention. I hope they're okay."

"Could the kittens have climbed out of the cage themselves?" Nancy asked.

"Impossible," Ms. Berman said. "Even though cats are great climbers, these babies are too small to get out of the cage. You'll see."

The girls followed Ms. Berman down a long, whitewashed hallway toward the cat area of the shelter. They came to a large, wooden door. "Here we are at the Cat Cave." Ms. Berman turned the knob to let them in.

"Achoo!" Bess started to sneeze even before Ms. Berman opened the door. "Achoo! Choo! Choo!" Ms. Berman handed Bess a tissue with a questioning look.

"I don veel very vell," Bess said, her nose growing more and more stuffy every second.

"Are you sick?" Ms. Berman asked, her voice suddenly tense.

"I'm not thick," Bess insisted. She blew her nose loudly. "Sick, I mean."

"She has allergies," George explained.

"Hmm," Ms. Berman said thoughtfully, handing Bess another tissue. "This worries me girls. You see, the baby kittens are very young and can catch germs easily. Just in case it's more than allergies, I think it would be better if you didn't go inside, Bess."

Bess's nose was starting to run, and her eyes felt itchy. "Go ahead. I'll meet you after the tour," she told Nancy and George. Bess practically ran through the shelter door, gasping for fresh air. Once outside she felt better immediately.

Nancy and George continued the tour with Ms. Berman.

The baby kittens were incredibly cute. Nancy and George took their time looking at them, watching as they slept. Ms. Berman told the girls the kittens had to be bottle-fed because they were still too young to eat food or drink water on their own. Nancy asked about the blankets along the bottom of the cage.

"We have to keep the babies warm," Ms. Berman told them. "Usually the mother cat would care for the babies, but since their mama left them behind a store downtown, I suppose I'm their mother now." She yawned. "I must say, no matter how sweet these little ones are, these babies are simply exhausting to take care of." She yawned once more.

"Who—," Nancy began, but before she finished her question, Ms. Berman's cell phone rang.

While Ms. Berman took the call, Nancy and George looked around the Cat Cave. There was just the one door. A supply shelf in the back was stacked with bottles, bags, and boxes. Rows of cat cages were set up along the walls. They were stacked in threes on top of one another, all the way up to the high windows. Every cage had a least one cat in it.

The baby kittens were in an open-topped glass cage like the one at Pete's Pet Shop. Ms.

Berman was clearly right; they were too small to climb out on their own. Nancy was certain that someone must be taking them. But who? And why?

Ms. Berman was still talking on her cell phone. She'd moved away from Nancy and George now and was talking in a lowered voice, but her words echoed inside the room. She probably didn't know it, but the girls could hear her whole side of the phone conversation.

"Yes," Ms. Berman said. "You want one more?" Pause. "I guess I can take it," Ms. Berman replied to whatever the other person asked. She fell quiet for a long minute before ending the call, saying, "Okay. I'll be right there."

Snapping her phone shut, Ms. Berman crossed to where the girls were standing, near the kitten cage.

"I have to run," she said, suddenly shuffling the girls toward the Cat Cave door.

"We were hoping to check out the shelter exits and the Dog Dorm," Nancy said.

"I'm sorry. We'll have to finish the tour later. Can you come back tomorrow?" Ms. Berman asked. "There's something I've got to take care of right away."

Nancy had one last pressing question, which she tried to ask as Ms. Berman escorted her and George out the front door of the shelter. "We still need to know—"

But Ms. Berman didn't pay attention to Nancy. Without saying "Good-bye," she turned rapidly on her heel and disappeared back into the building.

"Well, that was odd," George said to Nancy as they walked away from the shelter.

"What was odd?" Bess asked, coming over from the bench where she'd been waiting.

"Ms. Berman." Nancy explained how the shelter director couldn't stop yawning and then rushed away after the strange call came.

Nancy pulled out her notebook. She wanted to jot down a few things to consider later. She wrote a big heading that read QUESTIONS at the top of the page. That's when Suzie Park came out of the shelter. She was proudly wearing her River Heights Animal Shelter jacket, even though it was another warm day.

"What're you doing here?" Suzie asked the Clue Crew.

George explained that they were investigating the missing kitten mystery. "Have you seen or heard anything?" George asked.

"Me? No," Suzie said firmly. "But I've been

working so hard this week, I haven't had time to talk much with the other volunteers," Suzie explained. "Today I fed all the animals and then walked all the dogs." She yawned. "Boy, am I tired! I'm headed home for a nap. It'll be another busy day tomorrow."

Nancy stopped Suzie before she ran off. "Hey Suzie! Did you know you've got white speckles on your shelter jacket." Then she asked, "Did you spill something on it?"

Suzie glanced down, a surprised look crossing her face. Then after a pause she replied, "Oh drat! Milk must have splattered when I was feeding the cats. Thanks for pointing it out, Nancy. I'll wash it off at home." She smiled, readjusting the sleeve of her coat.

"No problem," Nancy said, glad she'd mentioned it.

"I desperately want to see the kittens," Bess told Nancy and George after Suzie had gone. "How about if we go back in and I plug my nose?"

"You'll probably still sneeze," George said. Then a lightbulb went on in George's head. "What if we hold you up outside and you look in through the Cat Cave window?"

"Great idea!" Bess was excited.

The girls moved to the back of the shelter building.

Nancy and George got on their hands and knees in the grass under the window, forming little tables with their bodies. Bess climbed on top of her best friends. She peeked through the glass. "Hey, George," she said, "I see Ms. Berman in there, but where are the kittens?"

"Middle of the room," George said, groaning under Bess's weight. "In an open glass cage."

"Oh there they are," Bess proclaimed after a short search. "They are sooo cute! You know, they look almost exactly like the ones at Pete's Pet Shop!"

As Bess went on and on about how sweet they were, Nancy heard a squeaking noise. She raised her head slightly to identify where the sound was coming from and saw Ms. Berman coming out the back door of the shelter. Forgetting that she was supporting Bess, Nancy jumped up, calling, "Ms. Berman! Wait up!"

Bess fell, knocking into a surprised George. Nancy left her friends tangled in a pile of arms and legs and ran after Ms. Berman. Nancy

caught up to the shelter director at her car where she was loading a small box into her back seat. The box said KIND KITTENS on the side.

"Ms. Berman," Nancy spoke rapidly, seeing that Ms. Berman was in a huge hurry to leave. "Who found the orphaned kittens?"

Ms. Berman climbed into the driver's seat of her sedan, saying, "Mrs. Sheila Simon." Nancy knew who that was.

After Ms. Berman sped away, Bess and George came over.

"What was that all about?" Bess asked, looking at Nancy sternly. A grass stain on Bess's T-shirt matched the grass stains on George's pants.

"Oh my goodness! I'm so sorry times ten," Nancy told her friends, her hands covering her mouth. "I forgot you were up there, and I needed to ask Ms. Berman one last question. Now I know where we've got to go next. Let's find Hannah. We're moving on."

"Where are we going?" the cousins asked at

the same time, quickly forgiving Nancy for her absentmindedness.

"Downtown. Near Pete's Pets, there's a book store called the Book Nook," the young detective replied. "In order to solve this mystery we need to interview the owner of that store, Mrs. Sheila Simon."

CHAPTER FOUR

Quick Questions

The girls found Mrs. Simon standing on a step-ladder, getting a book for an older customer.

George leaned over to her friends and whispered, "She looks like a character from a scary book." Nancy and Bess laughed quietly. Sure enough, Mrs. Simon had gray hair, piled high in a bun, and tight, leathery skin. The girls would have been afraid of her if it weren't for Mrs. Simon's sweet smile and friendly greeting.

"Hello there, young ladies," she said formally, climbing carefully down the ladder.

Nancy returned the greeting, then explained, "We heard you found the baby kittens that are now at the shelter. May we ask you a few questions about them?"

"Of course," Mrs. Simon said, handing her customer the book and showing him to a small reading table. She then led the girls into her office, a dark and gloomy room with books stacked tightly on floor-to-ceiling shelves. "Tea?"

"No thank you," Nancy replied, pulling out her detective's notebook. "Please tell us about the kittens you found."

"Well," Mrs. Simon began, "I was leaving through the back door one afternoon, heading to my car in the alley, and I practically stepped on the poor little darlings! All six babies were in a cardboard box just off to the side of my doorstep. They were so tiny." Cupping her hands in a ball, Mrs. Simon showed the girls just how small the kittens were. "I was very worried about them, so I called Ms. Berman at the shelter. She picked them up almost immediately."

"What about the mother cat?" Bess asked. "Did you see her around?"

"Oh goodness, no," Mrs. Simon replied. "I would have sent her with the babies. They need their mother."

Nancy shut her notebook, and Bess thanked Mrs. Simon for her time.

"I'm curious," George said to the woman, as they were leaving the office, "can we please see where you found them?"

"Certainly," Mrs. Simon said. "I'll let you out the back way."

The girls were in the alley looking at the doorstep where the kittens had been found when the back door to the next store over suddenly opened. A short, round man, with very little hair came into the alley carrying a bag full of trash.

"Who are you? And what are you girls doing poking around back here?" he asked, suspiciously.

"I'm Nancy Drew," Nancy replied, "and these are my friends Bess and George. We're investigating some missing kittens."

"I don't know about missing kittens," the man said, tossing his trash bag into a Dumpster. "I heard a cat meow back here once, but that was about a week ago." After a moment of silence while the girls continued looking around, the man said, "Hey, detective girls, maybe you can help me out with *my* mystery."

"You have a mystery?" Bess asked.

"Yeah," he replied. "I'm a candle maker and I use pure, white, cotton rags to clean up. Last week, I washed a dozen and hung them to dry on my windowsill." He pointed to the window at the back of his shop. "When I went to bring in my rags, they were gone. Solve that one."

"Interesting. I promise we'll keep an eye out for them," Nancy assured him.

"Let me know if you find anything," the man said, then went back into his store.

"Yesterday we had no mysteries. Since then we've solved one and still have two more!" Bess exclaimed, fully amazed. "I say, let's keep working on the missing shelter kittens. After we solve that mystery, we can come back and search for the rags. At this rate, we'll never be bored again!"

"Great plan. I think we should go to Nancy's house now," George suggested. "I'd like to type up a list of questions about the kittens on her computer."

Walking out of the alley, toward their meeting

place with Hannah, the girls were surprised to find Chief McGinnis standing in front of Pete's Pets.

"How's the investigation going?" Nancy asked, one detective to another.

"A third kitten disappeared from the shelter today," he replied, shaking his head. "Still can't figure out who's taking them."

Chief McGinnis saw that Nancy was holding her notebook. "You girls find any clues?"

There was an awkward moment of silence before Bess jumped in saying, "Not quite yet."

"We're going to Nancy's house now to process what we've found so far," George explained.

"Let me know if you figure it out." Chief

McGinnis thanked the girls for their help and went inside Pete's shop.

Hannah brought them back to the house, where the girls hurried up to Nancy's bedroom. George sat at the computer desk, while Nancy reviewed her notes.

"We have a few possible suspects already," Nancy reported, surprising the other two.

George opened a blank document and typed as Nancy talked.

"Well," Nancy began, "First, there's Pete."

"Oh, right," Bess said, understanding immediately. "There were two kittens missing from the shelter and two kittens in his store. They looked a lot alike."

"Then," Nancy went on, "there's Mr. Jones, from Kind Kittens. He's the guy who Pete said is bringing the kittens to him."

"Got him." George said, typing quickly.

"Next, Ms. Berman was acting weird today. I think she's a suspect too." Nancy told George to write down the shelter manager's name. "Ms. Berman said on that phone call that she was going to take 'one more.' Maybe she meant one more *kitten*." Nancy closed her notebook.

"I saw her in the Cat Cave through the window, remember? And Chief McGinnis just said there was another kitten missing," Bess put in, adding to Nancy's information.

George made the case against Ms. Berman even stronger when she added, "Ms. Berman was rattling on about how the kittens take too much of her time. Maybe, she's getting rid of them one or two at a time."

Nancy thought a minute, then added, "The box in Ms. Berman's car said Kind Kittens on the side. Could she be giving the kittens to Mr. Jones, who then gives them to Pete?"

"The clues add up. I think we've solved this mystery!" Bess announced. "Obviously Ms. Berman took the kittens." Bess snatched up the phone. "What's the number for the police station?"

ChaPTER FiVE

Real Research

Nancy and George looked at Bess, surprised by her quick judgment.

George told Bess to hang up the phone for a minute while she printed out their list of suspects. "It sure does seem like Ms. Berman's the thief," George said, inspecting her work, then handing it to Nancy.

Nancy looked over the list, narrowing her eyes as she read. She was quiet for a short time, then said, "Don't call Chief McGinnis yet, Bess. I'm not totally convinced that Ms. Berman took the kittens. Let's do some research first. Maybe finding out how to care for baby kittens will help with this mystery," Nancy suggested.

George turned back to the computer and opened a search page. She typed in the site for the River Heights Animal Shelter. With Bess and Nancy reading over her shoulder, George discovered a tremendous amount of information on caring for new pets.

"It says that orphaned kittens need to be fed a special formula with a bottle." Bess pointed at a photo of a little hair ball being given white formula. She read the caption. "Babies must eat every two to three hours, even at night, to grow properly."

Nancy read the next part. "Kittens need warm blankets to sleep on and because they aren't ready for a litter box, someone has to clean up after them." Scratching her chin, Nancy went on, "Usually the mama cat would provide everything the new kittens need, but abandoned babies require lots of human help."

George scrolled down the web page. "At about four weeks old," she read, "the kittens will sleep through the night. Then, they can eat a mixture of cat food and formula. Or cat food and water. They can also use a litter box. All kittens reach these goals at slightly different ages."

"So?" Bess asked, looking over at Nancy. "Did you find what you're looking for?"

"I'm not sure yet . . . ," Nancy said. She was being quiet. The detective wheels were spinning inside her head.

"All the clues still lead to Ms. Berman," Bess said firmly, trying to push Nancy along.

"I know, I know," Nancy replied. "Ms. Berman is suspect number one. I just want to be absolutely certain before we accuse her. For some reason it just doesn't feel right to me yet."

"I hope whoever's taking the kittens knows what to do with them," George remarked.

"I feel pretty confident that the babies are fine," Nancy said. "All three of our suspects—Pete, John Jones, and Ms. Berman—definitely know how to care for baby kittens."

"So when can we call the police?" Bess asked,

her mind locked on suspect number one. "If we wait another day, Ms. Berman might steal even more kittens. Chief McGinnis said that three are gone already."

Nancy thought about that. It was a really good point. On the one hand, it seemed like Ms. Berman was clearly the thief. But on the other hand, Nancy's detective sense told her not to jump to a conclusion too fast.

"Know what would help me think more clearly?" Nancy asked the Clue Crew. "A double-fudge ice cream sundae!"

The cousins laughed.

"Nancy, I didn't know you thought with your stomach!" Bess giggled. "But I'm with you, especially if it has nuts on top."

"Personally, I think it's even better with maraschino cherries," George said, dreamily licking her lips.

While Bess tied her shoelaces, Nancy checked the time and realized that the ice cream shop was closing in thirty minutes. "We better hurry if we're going to solve this mystery today," she said, smiling.

Hannah was spending her free time over at Mr. Seilsopour's, so the girls headed next door. When the girls asked for a ride, Hannah agreed, but by the time she put her tools away there was only fifteen minutes before the shop closed.

They hopped out of Hannah's car and ran toward the ice cream store door. Just as they were about to go in, Pete from Pete's Pets came out, carrying a chocolate chunk, two-scoop cone.

"How's the mystery business?" Pete asked Nancy. "Chief McGinnis said you were helping him out."

"We're zeroing in on one particular suspect," she replied, looking past Pete and into the cool shop.

"Let me know when you catch the thief," Pete said, taking a bite from his cone.

"We want to come see your kittens again," Nancy told him.

"Well luck is on your side. I got another baby kitten this afternoon." Pete grinned. "He's a cutie." Pete wiped his mouth with a napkin and added, "I just closed up for the day, but you girls can come by tomorrow and see him, if you want."

George looked at Bess and Nancy. It was clear that they were all thinking the same thing: Another kitten went missing from the shelter yesterday, and Pete now had another kitten.

Could Pete be suspect number one? Or was it possible that he didn't know his kittens were the missing ones?

"We'll be there first thing in the morning," Nancy said with certainty.

"I can't join you," Bess said, regret in her voice. "Allergies."

"Sorry about that," Pete said to Bess, "but I'll teach Nancy and George how to bottle-feed the babies. It's so sweet the way they curl up in your hand." There was a dreamy look on Pete's face. He obviously loved those kittens.

Pete headed toward his shop and the girls turned to finally go into the ice cream store. But just as George put her hand on the door, the teenager who ran the shop flipped the sign from OPEN to CLOSED.

"Oh no!" Bess exclaimed. "Without ice cream to inspire us, we'll never be able to name the culprit!"

"I have an idea," George told the girls. "Why don't we ask Hannah to take us to the River

Heights Café tomorrow morning? They have awesome ice cream, including double-fudge sundaes. The best part is, they're open for breakfast before Pete's Pets opens up."

"Pancakes and ice cream for breakfast?" Nancy said, liking her lips. "Yum!"

"We can ask Hannah if it'll work to eat breakfast first, then drop me and Nancy off at Pete's, and then Bess can go work with Mr. Seilsopour on his truck." George summed up. "We'll call Hannah from Pete's when we need a ride again."

"A perfect plan," Nancy agreed.

"We'll solve this mystery tomorrow," Bess said. "For sure!"

ChaPTER Six

The Perfect Plan

"I'll have a double-chocolate-fudge sundae with extra whipped cream," Nancy told the waitress at the River Heights Café.

The waitress gave Nancy a funny look. "Are you sure you don't want eggs?"

"No, thanks. I need to think," Nancy said, as if that explained her odd breakfast order.

"I'll take a superscoop vanilla bean sundae," Bess ordered.

The waitress turned to George, who was sitting in the booth next to her cousin. "I suppose you want ice cream too?"

"Oh, yes," George told her. "If we are going to solve this mystery today, I need a banana split."

The waitress okayed their orders with Hannah, who was reading the morning paper and sipping a cup of coffee at the next booth. Hannah assured the waitress that the girls had promised to eat healthily for the rest of the day.

Shaking her head, the waitress took their orders and went into the kitchen.

"Okay," Bess said to Nancy after their unusual breakfast was delivered. "It's time to solve this case. I still think it's Ms. Berman."

"Well one thing seems pretty certain," Nancy said, licking whipped cream off her spoon. "The kittens at Pete's sure look a lot like the shelter kittens and the number of kittens that are missing from one place and appearing at the other place certainly seem to match up."

The girls talked about the clues and the suspects for a while longer, but they were interrupted when Ned Nickerson, a fourth-grade boy from school, came into the café.

"Scoot over, Nancy Drew," Ned said, squishing into the booth next to Nancy. "My mom dragged me along with her this morning," he said pointed at Mrs. Nickerson, sitting with some of her friends. "Thank goodness you three are here so I don't have to sit with her and her knitting club."

Ned ordered a glass of milk and a muffin from the waitress who had come to check on the girls and their desserts.

"Did you guys know that Deirdre Shannon got a new pet cat?" Ned asked his friends. The girls were surprised but held their comments until after the waitress returned with Ned's order.

"We just saw Deirdre at the pet store two days ago," Bess told Ned. "She was looking at dogs, not cats."

Ned took a gulp of his milk. "That's weird because I was walking by her house yesterday, and I heard meowing and she didn't used to have a pet." Ned commented.

"Are you positive?" Nancy's detective sense told her that there was something suspicious about Deirdre getting a cat when they all knew she wanted a beagle puppy.

"One hundred percent," Ned told them.

"I've got to write this down." Nancy reached into her back pocket for her purple detective's notebook. Her elbow accidentally knocked into Ned's glass, spilling the last bit of milk onto his blue soccer jacket.

"Oh, I'm so sorry," Nancy said, reaching for some napkins.

It wasn't a bad spill so Ned said, "No worries. It'll dry clear. Milk usually does—unlike yogurt or chili," Ned added, pointing out a gray speck then a brown spot on his coat.

"Ewww," Nancy said, handing him the napkins. "You seriously need to clean that coat."

"Why?" Ned shrugged. "I'll just spill something else on it tomorrow."

"Good point," George said with a giggle.

When Ned and his dirty jacket left the restaurant, it was still too early for either the pet store or car repair. All three girls agreed that they should head over to Deirdre's to check out her new cat since she lived close by. Hannah could stay and enjoy her paper a little longer, and they could walk there and back on their own.

As they left the restaurant, Chief McGinnis was coming in.

"Solved the mystery yet?" he immediately asked the girls.

"The ice cream we just ate is helping us focus," Nancy said. "We're off to investigate a bit more now."

"Ice cream for breakfast?" Chief McGinnis asked.

George smiled. "Eat dessert first, that's my motto!"

"Sounds delicious," the chief said, thoughtfully. "Maybe I'll have ice cream too." The girls were about to leave when the chief suddenly stopped them. "All this talk about frozen treats, I nearly forgot to tell you—when Ms. Berman returned from a quick coffee run this morning, the last three kittens were gone."

ChaPTER SeVEN

Searching the Suspects

"All six are missing now," Nancy said thoughtfully as the girls headed toward Deirdre's house.

"Yikes!" George grabbed Nancy's arm just in time. Nancy was concentrating so hard, she'd nearly walked right into a fire hydrant.

"If Ms. Berman is in there feeding them every two hours, it doesn't give someone a lot of time to steal them, does it?" Nancy said, half to herself, half to the others.

"Just another reason why Ms. Berman is our main suspect," Bess said. "She has the most opportunity." Then Bess sneezed. "Achoo!" They had arrived at Deirdre's front door. "Yep, Deirdre has a cat all right." She rubbed her eyes and sneezed again.

"I can't believe you're sneezing before we even ring the doorbell!" George exclaimed. "You are *really* sensitive."

"I think it's getting worse," Bess said. "It's like I can sense a cat a mile away."

Nancy rang the doorbell at Deirdre's, while Bess stayed back on the sidewalk.

"Hi," Deirdre greeted the girls. "What's up?"

"Hey, Deirdre. We've got a weird question for you. . . . Ned said that you just got a pet cat. Is that true?" George asked.

"We thought you wanted a beagle," Bess called out.

"I don't have any pets *yet*," Deirdre replied. "My dad said he'll go look at Sunrise tonight after work." Deirdre crossed her fingers, hopefully.

"Ned must have been wrong—," Nancy began, but then she noticed something odd. Leaning forward, Nancy peered into Deirdre's hair. "What is that?"

Deirdre ran her fingers over her curly black hair and removed a green leaf. "Oh," she said, "it's nothing. I've been outside, feeding a stray cat. About a week ago, I found a cat in my backyard. It looked hungry, so my mom said I could give it some tuna." Deirdre pointed at the tuna she'd just put out, by the base of a big, leafy tree. "Now the hungry kitty comes by to eat every day, at about the same time." Deirdre checked her watch. "She should be here any minute."

"Achoo!" Bess sneezed.

"Shhh, you'll frighten her away," Deirdre warned. "She's a real scaredy-cat."

Bess plugged her nose, squeezing it tight.

It was only a minute or two before the cat showed up to eat. The girls watched as she gobbled down the tuna and then scampered off.

"I have a feeling that might be the shelter babies' mama," Nancy said. "Maybe she was out looking for food when Mrs. Simon called Ms. Berman. Mrs. Simon did say that Ms. Berman showed up really fast."

"The shelter kittens do look an awful lot like her," George added in agreement.

"After we find the kittens we should come and get her. Put the family back together," Bess said, finally releasing her nose.

"The cat's gone for today. She'll be back tomorrow though, I bet." Deirdre told them. "Well, I gotta go—I'm off to Natalie's house for a play date. Originally Suzie was supposed to come over and hang out, but she called to say she's way too tired and needs a nap. I hope she's not getting sick."

The girls waved good-bye to Deirdre, then turned and walked down the sidewalk together. They were off to get Hannah at the café so she could take Nancy and George to the pet store, then bring Bess to Mr. Seilsopour's to work on the truck.

Bess was so excited, she ran up the walkway to Mr. Seilsopour's house. There, she found Mr. Seilsopour laying out the tools he'd need for the day. The radio was turned up loud and a great tune was playing. It was all too perfect.

"You and Hannah are going to finish changing the other three tires," he told Bess, "while I replace the truck's battery."

"Hey!" Bess exclaimed, as they got to work, "This truck has no windows!" The places where the windows would have been were completely open and airy.

"I know," Mr. Seilsopour said. "I'm going to install new ones as soon as the car can be driven down to my shop. You can help put in the windows, too, if you want."

"I'd love to!" Bess cheered. Suddenly, Bess sneezed. "That's weird," she said to herself, looking around. "There are no cats anywhere. Hmm." Then, after sneezing again, Bess got busy, handing Hannah the tools she needed.

At Pete's Pets, Pete was supposed to be teaching George and Nancy how to feed the baby kittens, but there were so many people in the store, he was too busy.

"I've asked Mr. Jones to show you," Pete told them as he rang up a dog food sale.

"The name's John Jones," a large, gray-haired man wearing overalls told them, shaking hands with each of the girls. "And these babes are from my Kind Kittens farm. I brought the last few little guys in this morning."

George leaned over and whispered to Nancy, "He's one of our suspects."

"I know," Nancy replied softly.

"Let's get started." Mr. Jones picked up one of the kittens from the open-topped cage and tucked it in the palm of his hand. "The trick with newbies is to make sure they are getting enough formula to grow. These little babies are in a transitional stage," he said, shaking up a bottle that had a mixture of water and white creamy formula in it.

"How old are the kittens?" Nancy asked.

"Just over four weeks. I don't give away any kittens until they can sleep through the night. That's why Pete only gets one or two at a time. Each of these little guys progresses on their own timetable, so I hand 'em over when they're sleepin' well. Pete promises me he won't sell 'em until they can eat and drink on their own."

Nancy remembered the first time they'd seen

the kittens, Pete had told them that they weren't ready for adoption yet.

"Do you own the mama cat?" Nancy asked, in full detective mode.

Mr. Jones handed Nancy the kitten. "Hold this," he said and then pulled out his wallet. The photo pages were jammed with pictures. He flipped through the shots until he said, "Here she is. This is Gabriella. Pete's six kittens are her babies." The cat in the photo looked a lot like the cat they'd seen at Deirdre's, but this one had a big, black ring around her right eye.

The baby that Nancy now held had the same black ring around her eye. Nancy handed the baby to George and pulled out her notebook and pen. She quickly knocked Mr. Jones off the suspect list. He really did own the mama cat. That also meant that Pete was no longer a suspect, because these were obviously Gabriella's babies.

So Bess must be right after all. All the clues led back to Ms. Berman. But if she wasn't giving the kittens to Pete, who was she giving them to? All the clues swirled in Nancy's head until suddenly she realized—maybe there was another suspect, one they hadn't considered yet. . . .

"Did you say that Pete can't sell the kittens until they can eat food and drink water on their own?" Nancy asked.

"Yep," Mr. Jones confirmed.

"Not milk?" Nancy asked. George looked at her funny, unsure where Nancy was headed with her question.

"Kittens drink a white formula. Cats drink

water." Mr. Jones said. "Although people always think of feeding milk to cats, milk isn't actually very good for a cat."

"Aha!" Nancy practically shouted. "I know who has been taking the kittens from the shelter."

Chapter Eight

Kind Kittens

Nancy went running out of Pete's with George on her heels. George's mom, Mrs. Fayne, was doing errands downtown, so she offered to take the girls back to Nancy's when they were done. They were definitely done at Pete's and in a hurry to get back to Bess!

"Bess," Nancy shouted as she jumped out of Mrs. Fayne's car after the short ride. "Drop the tools! We gotta roll."

"Roll?" Bess asked, setting down a ratchet. "Where are we going?"

George threw open the door to her mom's car and hopped to the curb. "Nancy knows who has been taking the kittens," George announced.

Nancy had already told George her theory, so she let Bess guess by way of a game:

"Who knows her way around the shelter?" Nancy asked.

"Ms. Berman," Bess replied.

"*And* who is tired all the time, a clue that she is up all night with baby kittens," Nancy asked.

"Ms. Berman?" Bess replied, sounding less certain as she began to grasp where Nancy was headed.

"Baby kittens are fed formula, not milk. Spilled formula dries white, while milk dries mostly clear . . . so . . . who had speckles of spilled *formula* on her jacket?"

"Suzie Park!" Bess said as all the clues came together.

"Suzie fits all the clues," George agreed.

Bess told Mr. Seilsopour that she'd be back later. Then the Clue Crew walked quickly toward Suzie's house.

On the way Bess told Nancy and George about the work she was going to do on Mr. Seilsopour's truck. "He said I can help install the windows. How cool is that?" Bess also mentioned that she couldn't seem to stop sneezing at Mr. Seilsopour's house. "I think I better go to a doctor and have my nose checked," she said with a laugh. "Now I sneeze even when there aren't any cats around."

When they got to Suzie's house, George knocked on the door, and Suzie opened it. She was wearing a bathrobe and yawning, like she'd just woken up from a nap.

Nancy pulled out her detective's notebook and

said, "Suzie, you know that mystery we're investigating? Well, we've come to the conclusion that you're the one taking the shelter kittens."

Suzie's eyes grew really wide. "I . . . ," she sputtered. "I mean, I . . . ," she sputtered again. Finally, Suzie sighed deeply, her shoulders slumping. "Okay, I admit it. I took the kittens." Suzie looked like she was about to cry.

"Why?" Nancy asked, stashing her notebook back into her pocket.

"Well," Suzie said, wrapping her arms around herself, "I took them because I was worried. Ms. Berman was too tired—she's always complaining and stuff."

At that, George nodded. They'd heard Ms. Berman complain too.

"One morning, I saw her carrying a Kind Kittens box into the shelter, I thought she was going to put the kittens in that box and give them away." Suzie looked really serious. "Kittens can't be adopted until they can eat and drink on their own." Suzie led the girls through her house to the garage. "So, I've been taking care of them myself. I could only bring home one or two at a time, because that's all I could fit in my coat sleeves."

Nancy recalled how Suzie had been wearing her shelter coat even when it was hot outside.

"Taking care of all those kittens is really making me tired," Suzie said with a stretch and a yawn. "But it's worth it," she said, opening the garage door. "They are really cute and growing stronger every second!"

"Do your parents know?" Bess asked.

"Oh gosh, no!" Suzie replied. "I put the kittens in a box in the garage, and I tiptoe out every few hours to take care of them. I planned to sneak them all back into the shelter for adoption in a few more weeks."

"Achoo!" Bess began to sneeze again, so only Nancy and George went into the garage with Suzie.

"I made a nice warm bed under the window for the babies. I left the window open for fresh air and gave them my old baby blanket to keep warm," Suzie flipped on the light switch as she said, "All six little babies are right—"

Suzie screamed. Bess came running into the garage with her nose plugged.

"They're gone!" Suzie shrieked. "All the kittens are gone!"

ChaPTER NiNe

Cat Caper Closed?

Nancy whipped out her purple notebook. Apparently, she'd put it away too soon.

At the top of a blank page, Nancy wrote: *Clues*. Then she made a list of things that might apply to the case. What else had they learned over the past two days that might be important? Nancy thought and thought and thought.

Then, she wrote:

    1) The candle maker heard meowing behind
    Mrs. Simon's bookstore.
    2) The candle maker was missing his white
    rags.

3) Deirdre was feeding a stray cat, maybe even the mama cat.

4)

She left number four blank for a minute, while she wandered around the garage. The garage door had been closed, so how had the kittens escaped? Was someone else taking them? Nancy shook her head. There were no other suspects. And no one else knew that Suzie was hiding them.

Hmm. Nancy rubbed her chin. She was thinking hard.

Nancy looked at the cat bed again. Suzie really had made every effort to take good care of the kittens. Taking them from the shelter was wrong, but she'd done it only to protect them. The bed looked warm and comfy and there was a nice breeze coming through the open window. Nancy looked up at the window.

"Wait!" she said suddenly. "What's outside this window?" she asked Suzie.

"Just a tree," Suzie replied.

"That's a clue!" Nancy shouted. On her clues list, under number four, she wrote: *Open window.*

Nancy looked at her list and said, "It's just like in the movie. The mama cat rescued the baby by carrying it off in her mouth, though in this case she's not saving a beagle puppy. She's taking her own kittens."

"Are you sure?" Suzie asked, sniffling a little still but looking relieved that the babies weren't wandering around by themselves.

"I'm positive." Nancy shook her head firmly. "She must have left them alone for a moment, maybe to find herself some food, and when she got back, Mrs. Simon had already called the shelter. The babies were gone!"

"So, the cat has been looking around town for her babies?" George added questioningly. "We know she's been eating lunch at Deirdre's but doesn't stay long—it must be because she's on an important mission."

"And she found the kittens here!" Suzie

exclaimed. "The mama cat must have taken them out the garage window, getting in and out by climbing the tree. But . . ." Suzie's voice got real soft as she wondered, "Where did she take them?"

"The mama cat has been living somewhere while she searched for her babies," Nancy said, considering the possibilities. "It had to be somewhere warm. Sheltered, in case it rained. A place where she could bring the kittens once she found them all."

"Maybe in a box? Or under a bridge? Or—" George began to make a list.

"Achoo!" Bess interrupted with a loud sneeze.

"That's it, Bess!" Nancy exclaimed. "Bess's nose knows where the kittens are."

ChaPTER TEN

The Nose Knows

Suzie quickly got dressed and slipped on her favorite jacket. Then all the girls followed Nancy home.

"The kittens are at your house?" George asked, curiously, not understanding what Nancy had already figured out.

"Nope," Nancy passed right by her house and turned into Mr. Seilsopour's driveway. "The kittens are in Mr. Seilsopour's truck."

As if to prove it, Bess immediately sneezed.

Nancy explained her reasoning as the girls approached the truck. "Bess told us that Mr. Seilsopour's truck has no windows," Nancy said.

"Easy for a cat to climb inside," George said, nodding in agreement.

"The mama cat needed the candle maker's rags to make a nest—that's why they were missing," Nancy explained.

"Achoo!" Bess sneezed.

"And Bess, your sneezes are the most important clue of all!" Nancy said, opening the back door to Mr. Seilsopour's truck. There, on the backseat, snuggled up, toasty warm in the candle maker's clean rags, were all six baby kittens, happily sleeping next to their mama.

* * *

Ms. Berman and Chief McGinnis arrived at the house immediately after Nancy called them.

"The Clue Crew solved the case." Nancy explained how they'd worked together to follow the clues to Suzie's house and then again to the truck.

"Good work," Chief McGinnis said, shaking each of the girl's hands.

Ms. Berman looked at Suzie Park and said, "Suzie, if you felt like the kittens needed more attention, you should have talked to me about it."

Suzie lowered her eyes. "I'm so sorry for what I did," she replied sadly. "I bet you won't let me work at the shelter anymore." She took off her shelter jacket and handed it to Ms. Berman.

Ms. Berman refused it, saying, "Keep it Suzie. Even though you took the kittens when you shouldn't have, I know your heart was in the right place. I'd be happy to have you continue volunteering."

Suzie's eyes brightened. "I'll be the best worker you ever had," she said.

"I'm counting on it." Ms. Berman said with a small smile.

From her car, Ms. Berman pulled out an empty Kind Kittens box to place the babies in. "Yesterday, I delivered another bag of formula to Mr. Jones at his cat farm. Good thing I still have his empty box in my car."

Nancy nodded toward her two friends, now

understanding what Ms. Berman's phone call at the shelter had been about. Then Nancy pulled her friends into a hug, "We're an awesome team! The cat burglar caper is solved."

"I can't wait until we have another Clue Crew mystery," George said.

"Achoo!" Bess sneezed in agreement. "Achoo! Me too. Achoo!"

A Purr-Fect Puzzle

Finding the six kittens was a puzzle for Nancy Drew and the Clue Crew. In the end, they put together all the pieces to solve their mystery. Now you can make and solve your own purr-fect kitten puzzle too!

You will need:

White printer paper

Cardboard

Pencil and eraser

Markers, crayons, colored pencils

Glitter, stickers, and other decorations

Glue

Scissors

Pounce on these instructions:

❀ First use the pencil to draw some cute kittens on the white paper. Draw as many playful kittens as you like, and use the eraser if you want to change them along the way.

❀ Once you are set with your illustration, color it in with markers, crayons, and colored pencils. Add stickers, glitter and other decorations to bring the drawing to life. Use your imagination!

❀ When the drawing is done, and any glued on decorations are dry, glue the paper onto the cardboard. Be patient while this dries. If you do the last step too soon, your beautiful drawing could get messy.

❀ Finally, use your scissors to cut the picture into eight or ten pieces. Make the cuts wiggly in some places and with sharp-angled turns in others. Try not to cut only straight lines. Think about ways to make your puzzle challenging to put back together.

Now your puzzle is ready to be solved! You can make one with a friend and try to solve each other's kitten puzzles too.